# The Town Mouse and the Country Mouse

## Based on a story by Aesop

Retold by
Susanna Davidson

Illustrated by Jacqueline East

Reading Consultant: Alison Kelly
Roehampton University

There was once a little brown country mouse.

His name was Pipin.

He lived in a
house in a hedge.

In spring, he lay in the
grass and listened to
the birds sing.

In summer, he nibbled on wild strawberries...

...and cut grass for his winter bed.

One day, as the weather grew colder and a chill wind blew...

...he heard a **Tap! Tap! Tap!** at his door.

"Pipin!" called a voice.
"It's your cousin. I've
come to stay!"

Pipin flung open the door.

"Toby Town Mouse!"
he cried. "Come in!"

Pipin made Toby a seat
from soft, squashy moss.

"It's too damp!" said
Toby Town Mouse.

Pipin took Toby
on a walk.

Atishoo!

Smell the
flowers!

But the flowers
made him sneeze.

11

That night, Pipin went
to his food store.

He picked out his
best nuts and berries.

"Urgh!" said Toby Town Mouse. "I hate nuts."

"Is this all you have?
In town, we eat like kings."

13

"Really?" asked Pipin.
"Come and see for
yourself," said Toby.

"The country is horrible.
You'll never want to live
here again."

The next day, the
cousins woke at dawn.

"We'll take the train,"
said Toby.

They ran to the station.

Soon, they heard the
rattle tattle of pebbles,
jumping on the railway line.

"The train's coming!"
cried Pipin. "It's HUGE."

It came to a stop
with a screech and a snort.

17

A door flew open.
"Jump!" said Toby.

The train gave a shriek
and a snort and...

...it was off again.

Chugga-chugga-chugga-
chugga. Choo! Choo!

Pipin looked out of the
window. He could see trees
waving their branches.

Then there were
no trees at all – just tall
buildings touching the sky.

As the sky grew dark, the train stopped again.

Toby twitched his whiskers. He sniffed the air.

"We're here!" he said. "At last – I'm in town again."

Home, sweet home.

"Now follow me."

23

Toby leaped onto
the train platform.

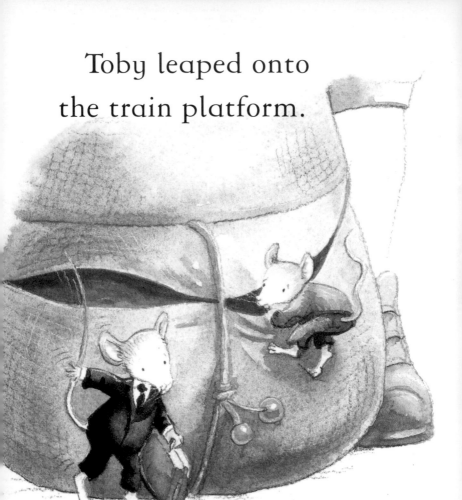

"Be quick, Pipin!" he
called. "Watch out for
stamping feet."

The mice ran
out of the station
and onto a busy street.

25

Pipin gasped. There was so much noise.

VROOM

The cars **vroomed.**
Their horns beeped.

And the smells! Pipin sniffed his first sausage and coughed on the smoke.

"And this," said Toby proudly, pointing his paw, "is my house."

He crept in through a small hole. Pipin followed.

They ran down dark
corridors under the floor...

...and up secret stairs
behind the walls.

They danced across the
empty ballroom...

30

...and played with toys in the children's nursery.

"Race you to the dining room," said Toby.

"Time for a feast!"

The mice jumped
onto the table and
began to eat.

They nibbled on pie.
They licked up cream.

33

Toby ate his way
through the cheese...

...while Pipin
dipped his paw
in chocolate
sauce.

"Gosh!" said Toby.
"I'm nearly full."

Pipin clutched his tummy.
"I think... hic... I'm going
to be... hic... sick."

Suddenly, the table shook.
Toby turned.

"It's the cat!" he cried.

"Hello," purred the cat,
licking her lips.

*My* dinner
time, I think...

Toby grabbed Pipin.
"Come on!" he said.

They darted
this way
and that.

Pounce! Pounce!
went the hungry cat.

She knocked over
a jug and it crashed
to the floor.

"Quick!"
Toby called.
"Into this hole."

Pipin ran. The cat
leaped. She swiped at
Pipin with her
pointy claws...

...and missed.
"Drat!" she hissed.

Pipin dropped to the
floor. "Oh cousin!" he said.
"I want to go home."

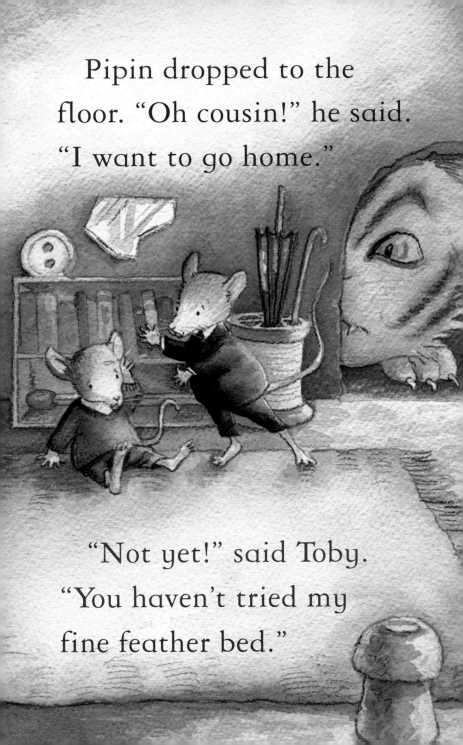

"Not yet!" said Toby.
"You haven't tried my
fine feather bed."

But the next morning,
Pipin still wanted to leave.
Toby gave him a map to
the station.

"Goodbye!"
said Pipin.

Pipin ran to the station.
He danced in and out of
the stamping feet...

...and hid in a bag
to get on the train.

In the starry dark,
Pipin finally reached
his hedge.

Home, sweet
home!

He sniffed the sweet,
cold air and smiled.

Then he snuggled
down in his warm
hay bed.

"This is the life for me,"
he said.

*The Town Mouse and the Country Mouse* is one of Aesop's Fables. These are a collection of short stories first told in Ancient Greece around 4,000 years ago. Beatrix Potter retold the story in *The Tale of Johnny Town Mouse.*

Series editor: Lesley Sims
Designed by Louise Flutter

First published in 2007 by Usborne Publishing Ltd., Usborne House, 83-85 Saffron Hill, London EC1N 8RT, England. www.usborne.com
Copyright © 2007 Usborne Publishing Ltd.